The l
r

12

2

BLACKDOG
LEVI PINFOLD

For my family,
and families in general

A TEMPLAR BOOK

First published in the UK in 2011 by Templar Publishing
This softback edition published in 2012 by Templar Publishing,
an imprint of The Templar Company Limited,
Deepdene Lodge, Deepdene Avenue, Dorking, Surrey, RH5 4AT, UK
www.templarco.co.uk

Copyright © 2011 by Levi Pinfold

This book was painted in tempera on paper,
using both self-prepared and pre-mixed paint.

2 4 6 8 10 9 7 5 3

ISBN 978-1-84877-748-4

Edited by Libby Hamilton

Printed in Italy

BLACKDOG

LEVI PINFOLD

templar publishing

 One day, a black dog came to visit the Hope family. Mr Hope was the first to see it.

"My goodness!" he cried, dropping his toast. He didn't waste any time in phoning the police.

"There's a black dog the size of a tiger outside my house!" he told the policeman.

The policeman laughed.

"What should I do?" asked Mr Hope.

"Don't go outside," said the policeman, and put down the phone.

 Mrs Hope was next to get up.

"My goodness!" she cried, dropping her mug of tea. She didn't waste any time in calling for Mr Hope.

"Did you know there's a black dog the size of an elephant outside?" she yelled.

"Yes," said Mr Hope.

"What should we do?" asked Mrs Hope.

"Turn out the lights so it doesn't know we're here!"

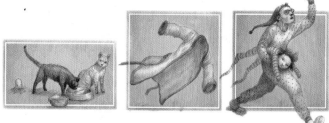

 Adeline Hope was next to get up.

"My goodness!" she cried, dropping her toothbrush. She didn't waste any time in calling for her parents.

"Did you know there's a black dog the size of a Tyrannosaurus rex outside?"

"Yes," said Mr and Mrs Hope together.

"What should we do?" asked Adeline.

"Close the curtains so it can't see us."

Maurice Hope was next to get up.

"My goodness!" he cried, dropping his teddy. He didn't waste any time in calling for the family.

"Did you know there's a black dog the size of a Big Jeffy outside?"

"What's a Big Jeffy?" asked Adeline Hope.

"Never mind that! What should we do?" demanded Maurice Hope.

"Hide under the covers!" they wailed.

 It was then that the youngest member of the Hope family, called Small (for short), noticed that there was something going on.

"What are you lot doing under there?"

"We're hiding from the Black Dog!" they whispered.

"Oh, you are such sillies," said Small, opening the front door.

"Don't go out there!" gasped her family.

"The hound will eat you up!"

"It'll munch your head!"

"It'll crunch your bones!"

But Small had gone anyway.

Outside, the Black Dog leaned
down towards her and BREATHED.
  "Crikey, you ARE big!"
said Small. "What are you
doing here, you guffin?"
  The Black Dog
SNUFFED
at her.

 "All right then," she said. "If you're going to eat me, you'll have to catch me first." And with that she scurried into the lowering trees. As she ran, she made up a song:

"You can't follow where I go,
unless you shrink, or don't you know?"
  The Black Dog followed…

 As Small hurried towards the frozen pond,
under the little bridge and over the ice, she sang:

"You've got fat legs, ice is thin,
lose some weight or you'll fall in."
And the Black Dog followed…

 Next she scuttled through the playground, down the slide and around the roundabout, singing:

"You've a BIG TUM, I'm all slim,
you'll fit through if you're more trim."
      And still the Black Dog followed…

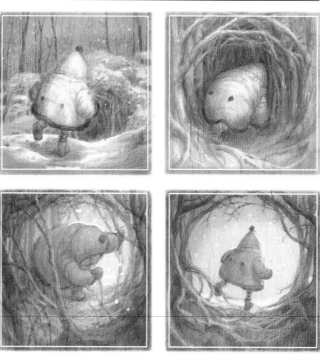

 Finally, Small had run all the way back to the house.

"You'll find out why they all hide, if you follow me inside."

And with that, Small tumbled into her warm home through the cat flap. She really was that small.

And so, by now, was the Black Dog.

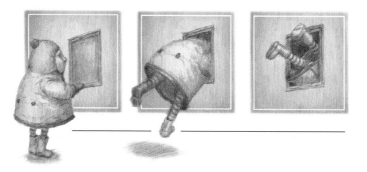

 Inside, Small grabbed a
washing basket and, as the
Black Dog scrabbled in behind
her, she covered him with a loud "HA!"

Just then, the rest of the Hope family
popped up from behind their barricade.

"You haven't been munched!" cried
Mrs Hope.

"You haven't been crunched!" cheered
Mr Hope.

"You haven't been eaten!" yelled Maurice
Hope (missing a poetic opportunity).

"But where's the Black Dog?" asked Adeline.

Without a word, Small lifted the basket.

 The rest of the Hope family were extremely pleased to see that the Black Dog was neither so huge, nor so scary, as they had feared.

"He doesn't seem fierce at all now I really look at him," said Mr Hope. The rest of the family agreed.

"We were silly," said Adeline. "Only Small knew the right thing to do."
Everyone was quiet for a while, thinking how brave Small had been.
   "You've got a lot of courage, facing up to a big, fearsome thing like
that," said Mrs Hope.

 "There was nothing to be scared of, you know," replied Small Hope as she went to sit by the fire.

And the Black Dog followed.